Chapter 1

Chris didn't like computers. Of course, he didn't say so.

His friends were good on computers. Najma was brilliant, but she had a computer at home. Chris didn't.

Gizmo and Najma were fast on the keyboard. Chris was slow. He had to search for the keys. He was slow with the mouse.

Things went wrong for him. He couldn't use the tool bar. He couldn't open a file. He was no good at computer games.

Wolf Hill

I Hate Computers!

Roderick Hunt
Illustrated by Alex Brychta

Oxford University Press

Oxford University Press, Great Clarendon Street, Oxford, OX2 6DP

Oxford New York
Athens Auckland Bangkok Bogota Buenos Aires Calcutta
Cape Town Chennai Dar es Salaam Delhi Florence Hong Kong
Istanbul Karachi Kuala Lumpur Madrid Melbourne Mexico City
Mumbai Nairobi Paris São Paulo Singapore Taipei Tokyo
Toronto Warsaw

and associated companies in
Berlin Ibadan

Oxford is a trade mark of Oxford University Press

First Published 1998

ISBN 019 918658 8

Printed in Hong Kong

‘I just don’t get it,’ he thought. ‘I hate computers.’

Najma would say, ‘Let me do it,’ and Chris would let her. Najma made it look easy. Chris always got it wrong.

Then one day something went badly wrong with a computer - and everyone blamed Chris.

Chapter 2

Wolf Hill School has a computer room. Every week Miss Teal's class uses the computers.

Miss Teal wanted the children to make a newspaper. 'Work in groups,' she said. 'Work on the computer.'

Everyone liked the newspaper project. They all had ideas.

'We can have a joke page,' said Gizmo, 'and some puzzles.'

'And something about animals,' said Chris. 'I'd like to write about whales.'

'We could interview Mr Saffrey,' said Kat.

'What we want is some real news,' said Andy. 'We need something exciting.'

Everyone thought.

'It's no good,' said Kat. 'I just can't think of any news.'

'Of course not,' said Najma. 'You can't invent news. Something has to happen. Then it becomes a news story.'

Something did happen. It happened that afternoon.

Chapter 3

After school, Chris and Gizmo went home together. They walked down Wolf Street.

Chris sniffed the air. 'Can you smell something?' he said.

An old car was parked in the street. Petrol was dripping out of it. A trickle of petrol ran down the hill.

'Isn't that dangerous?' said Gizmo.

'Yes!' yelled Chris. He ran to the phone box at the end of the street.

'Come on!' he shouted. 'We must phone the fire station.'

Chris dialled 999. He asked for Fire. Then he told them about the petrol.

Gizmo waved at Chris. 'I'm going home to get my camera,' he said.

'Why?' called Chris.

'We've got a fire engine coming,' said Gizmo. 'How's that for some news!'

Chapter 4

The fire engine raced up. Its blue light was flashing. A crowd of people stopped to watch. Gizmo took lots of pictures.

Then the police came. They made everyone leave the street.

The fire engine spread powder under the old car. It soaked up the leaking petrol.

Nobody could go up Wolf Street.

'We can't get home,' said an old lady. 'I'm dying for a cup of tea.'

A policeman spoke to Chris. 'Did you phone for the fire engine?'

'Yes,' said Chris.

'Well done,' said the policeman. 'You did the right thing.'

'Would you both look this way, please?' said Gizmo.

'Why?' asked the policeman.

'I want to take a photograph. It's for our newspaper project.'

Chapter 5

Everyone was pleased with the news story. Chris was a hero.

Najma wrote about it. The story went on the front page of the newspaper. The headline said, 'Chris's Quick Thinking Saves Street!'

'That's brilliant,' said Andy.

Gizmo took the photographs to school. 'These are great,' said Kat. 'We can put them on the front page.'

Chris was pleased. 'I'm famous at last,' he said. 'I'm on the front page of a newspaper.'

‘Everyone will want a copy now!’ joked Gizmo.

‘That’s a good idea,’ said Najma.

‘What is?’ asked Loz.

‘If our newspaper is good, we can sell it,’ said Najma.

Chapter 6

At last the newspaper was finished. Miss Teal peered at the screen.

'It looks good,' she said. 'You've all worked hard.'

Najma wanted to print a copy.

'Sorry,' said Miss Teal. 'The printer is busy. Never mind. Just save it. You can print it next week.'

Kat and Najma told Miss Teal about their idea.

'Can we sell our newspaper?' they asked.

'What would you do with the money?' asked Miss Teal.

'We've thought of a good cause,' said Gizmo.

'Whales are in danger,' said Chris. 'I wrote about them in the newspaper.'

'We want to give the money to Whale Watch,' said Andy.

'What a good idea,' said Miss Teal.

Chapter 7

On Monday, Chris brought a sheet of paper to school.

'It's my story about whales,' he said. 'I want to change it.'

'You can't,' said Gizmo. 'It's too late.'

'We've finished the newspaper,' said Kat. 'Najma's the editor. We should ask her, but she's away.'

Najma wasn't at school.

'She must be ill,' said Loz.

Later, Chris went past the computer room. There was nobody in the room and the door was open.

'I'll just make one change to my Whale Watch story,' thought Chris. 'It should be easy.'

He went in and sat down at the computer. He switched it on and waited.

The screen came up. Then something terrible happened.

The computer made a loud noise.

'Phut,' it went. The screen went very bright. Then it went dead.

'Oh no!' said Chris. 'What have I done?'

Chapter 8

Chris was in trouble.

'You know the rules,' said Miss Teal. 'You must never use the computer room without permission.'

She looked at the computer.

'I don't know what you've done to it,' she said. 'It's just dead.'

Everyone was upset. They had worked hard on the newspaper. Now all the work was lost. Kat gave Chris an angry look.

Chris felt terrible. He tried not to cry. What was it about computers? No wonder he was scared of them.

'Everybody is angry with me now,' he thought. 'I hate computers.'

Then Gizmo saw something. He looked up at the ceiling.

There was a wet patch. Below it was a tiny drop of water. It shone like a pearl. It grew bigger.

Then it fell.

It dropped into the back of the computer.

Chapter 9

'There's a water tank in the roof,' said Mr Saffrey. 'It's been leaking all weekend.'

Chris felt much better. At least it wasn't his fault.

'I'm really sorry,' Mr Saffrey went on. 'Your work has been lost.'

Everyone was upset. 'All that effort,' said Andy.

At break time Najma came to school. 'I've been to the dentist,' she said.

Nobody spoke.

Najma looked at everyone. 'What's the matter?' she said.

'The computer has broken down,' said Kat. 'All our work is lost.'

Najma grinned. 'No, it isn't,' she said.

She took a floppy disk out of her bag. 'I made a back-up copy on Friday. I saved it on this disk.'

'So we can print the newspaper after all?' said Loz.

'Najma, I could kiss you,' said Chris.

'Yuk!' said Najma.